This Little Tiger book belongs to:

_____

_____

_____

For Henry, who likes Brown Bears
- S S

For Emma, a truly loyal and courageous friend, who challenges her greatest
fears every day with a punch, a kick, and a giggle
- C P

LITTLE TIGER PRESS LTD,
an imprint of the Little Tiger Group
1 Coda Studios, 189 Munster Road, London SW6 6AW
www.littletiger.co.uk

First published in Great Britain 2018
This edition published 2019

Text copyright © Steve Smallman 2018
Illustrations copyright © Caroline Pedler 2018
Steve Smallman and Caroline Pedler have asserted their rights to be identified as the author
and illustrator of this work under the Copyright, Designs and Patents Act, 1988

Printed in China • LTP/1400/2652/0219

2 4 6 8 10 9 7 5 3 1

Scaredy BEAR

Steve Smallman

Caroline Pedler

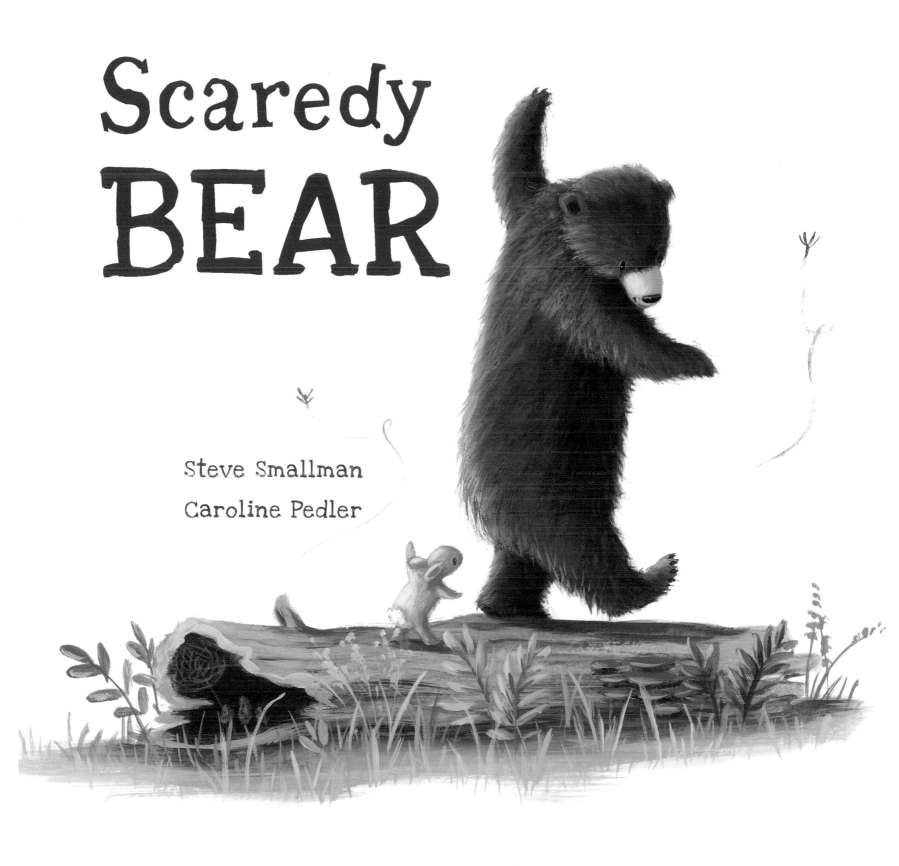

LiTTLE TiGER

LONDON

Little Bob was the bravest of bunnies.
He LOVED exploring, but he HATED going to bed.
"Oh why can't I go out and play?" he moaned.

"Because," said his mum,
"In the deep, dark forest there's nothing so scary
As the terrible creature they call the BIG HAIRY!
He's got huge scary teeth, and long scary claws,
And it sounds just like thunder whenever he roars!"

"Oooooooooooh!"
gasped Little Bob, jumping into bed,
where he stayed until . . .

. . . his mum was asleep!
Then he crept out of bed, grabbed
an extra pointy carrot, and set
off to find the BIG HAIRY!
The forest felt mean and
menacing in the moonlight.

"Perhaps I should look for the
Big Hairy another day," Little Bob
whispered to himself.

Then he spotted a shadow.
A shadow that looked
exactly like . . .

. . . AN OWL!

Quick as a flash, Little Bob
ran this way and that.

He dodged
and swerved,

and climbed
and **leapt,**

and just in time,
he dived under **a great, big bush!**
But it wasn't a bush.

It was a bear.

"EEEEK!" squeaked the bear. "You scared me!"
"Sorry!" said Little Bob. "I'm hunting for the Big Hairy!
In all of the forest there's nothing so scary
As the terrible creature they call the BIG HAIRY!"

"He sounds awful!" gasped the bear,
who didn't want to be on his own
if there was a monster around.
"Can I come with you?"

"OK," nodded the bunny.

"My name's Little Bob. What's yours?"

"I don't know," said the bear.

"What do your friends call you?"
asked Little Bob.

"I haven't got any friends," said the bear.

"Oh!" said Little Bob. "Well, I'll be
your friend if you like, and I will
call you . . . Big Bob!"

Big Bob was very
excited to have a friend.
"What do friends do?" he asked.
"This and that," Little Bob
said with a shrug.

So that's what they did
until Big Bob's tummy
started to rumble.

"Little Bob," he said, "do friends share their carrots?"
"Yes," said Little Bob, "but not *this* carrot. I'm going to stick *this* right up the Big Hairy's nose!"

"Gosh!" gulped Big Bob.
"How can you be so brave when you are so small?"
"Because," Little Bob whispered,
"I'm **big** on the inside."

"I must be tiny on the inside," sighed Big Bob.
"I'm sure there's a big bear in there somewhere,"
said Little Bob, looking in Big Bob's ear.
"You just need to let him out!"

Then Little Bob's tummy rumbled too.
"I'll get us some food," smiled Big Bob, ambling off.

It wasn't long before Little Bob heard a
noise behind him.

"That was quick!" he chuckled.
But it wasn't his friend.

It was a fox!

The fox **leaped** towards Little Bob,

and was about to gobble him up when . . .

...RoARRR!

Out from the bushes came a huge, hairy creature.

It had big scary teeth, and long scary claws,

And it made the ground shake with its thunderous roars.

The fox was so scared he raced
away into the trees.

"IT'S the BIG HAIRY!"
squealed Little Bob, shakily holding up
his extra pointy carrot.

Then the Big Hairy stopped roaring, gave a worried smile and said, "Are you all right, Little Bob?"

"Big Bob! It's you!"
cried Little Bob in surprise. "You're the Big Hairy!"

"I can't be," said Big Bob. "I'm just a scaredy bear."
"It's the big bear inside you," beamed Little Bob.
"You let it out!"

"Oh no!" gasped Big Bob.
"Does that mean . . ."

". . . you're going to stick your carrot up my nose?"

Little Bob looked up at his friend's worried face
and started to giggle. Then he started to laugh.
Soon Big Bob was laughing too.

And, when they were all laughed out, they shared the extra pointy carrot for supper.

"What shall we do now, Big Bob?" yawned Little Bob.

"I think it's time for you to go home," said Big Bob.

"But can we still be friends tomorrow?"

"Of course!" said Little Bob. "We can be friends forever!"
Big Bob smiled. Then the two friends wandered on,
chatting about this and that, all the way home to bed.

More brilliant books for bedtime from Little Tiger Press!

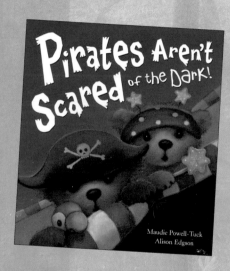

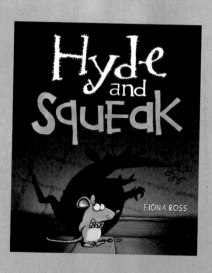

For information regarding any of the above titles
or for our catalogue, please contact us:
Little Tiger Press Ltd, 1 Coda Studios,
189 Munster Road, London SW6 6AW
Tel: 020 7385 6333
E-mail: contact@littletiger.co.uk
www.littletiger.co.uk